Mage
v-one
THE HERO DISCOVERED

BY MATT WAGNER

Mage
V-one

THE HERO DISCOVERED

Written and Illustrated
by Matt Wagner

Lettered by
Bob Pinaha

Edited by Kay Reynolds,
Gerry Giovinco and
Diana Schutz

STARBLAZE
GRAPHICS

THE DONNING COMPANY/PUBLISHERS
NORFOLK/VIRGINIA BEACH • 1987

Mage One—The Hero Discovered by Matt Wagner is one
of the many graphic novels published by The Donning
Company/Publishers. For a complete listing of our titles, please
write to the address below.

The Donning Company/Publishers
5659 Virginia Beach Boulevard
Norfolk, Virginia 23502

MAGE was originally published in comic book format by
Comico The Comic Company.

First printing March 1987

10 9 8 7 6 5 4 3 2 1

Library of Congress Cataloging-in-Publication Data

Wagner, Matt.
  Mage.
  1. Arthurian romances.   II. Title.
PN6727.W25M3   1987   741.5'973   86-4487
ISBN 0-89865-465-1 (pbk. v. 1)
ISBN 0-89865-467-X (lim. ed.)

Printed in the United States of America

intro

The first time I truly caught sight of Kevin Matchstick was at the waterfront along Penn's Landing, in Philadelphia. I happened to be doing some idle sketching, trying to let my thoughts roam free for ideas that I eventually intended to submit to the guys at Comico as part of what would be their initial breakthrough into the world of full-color comics. I remember two sketches I produced that day. One was of a punky-looking, poncho-ed, leg-wrapped, and generally spritely street magician. The other was of myself. Not my first self-portrait, this sketch caught my eye because of the way I had looked in the sketch. Tired, skeptical, and mundane. This is what I had been looking for. This is the side of myself that I had never been able to draw before. Like most illustrators with a fantasy background, my output up until now had been a touch cursory—that is, not internalized enough but mainly concerned with the flash around the rims. This, then, was my first sight of Kevin Matchstick.

When I next saw Kevin Matchstick, he had changed. Still remarkably earthy, he now wore the gaudiness and spectacle of his childhood fantasies on his very chest. Though he still looked out at the world through those jaded eyes, he was brave enough to wear his hopes out in the open. This time he had a black T-shirt with a white lightning bolt down the front. Here was the hero I was looking for. Inside myself.

I then began to realize that this was, indeed, the very place one should look to find one's heroes. Beyond the fluidity it would bestow on the creative processes, it helped me to activate a lot *of* myself. My views on heroes (or should we say activists?) and their commitments to both themselves and others is the voice and conception behind what I see as the **Mage** trilogy— **The Hero Discovered, The Hero Defined,** and **The Hero Denied.** To say more here would merely take away from the points I hope to explore through their creation. Therefore, may I say that, although there are times when I deeply wish I had never met Kevin Matchstick, I also realize that without his existence I would never have looked inward wherein lies the hero who lives within us all.

Thank you,
Matthew Wagner

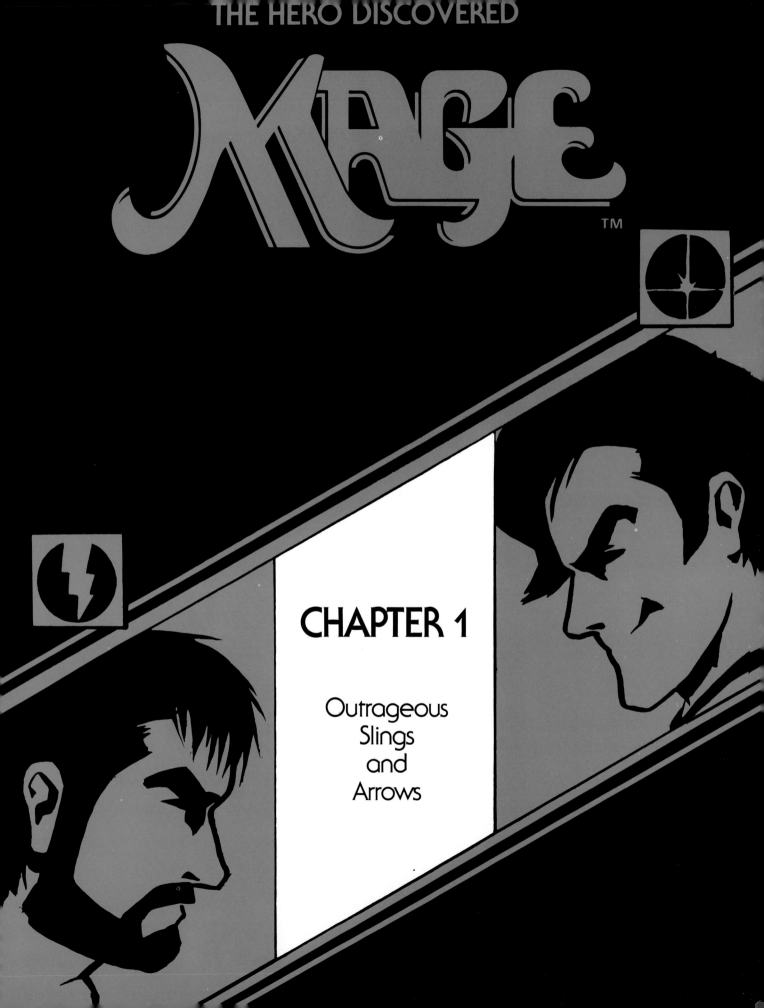

OH GREAT! A MUGGING. JUST WHAT I WANTED TO SEE TONI—

HEY!

HEY!!

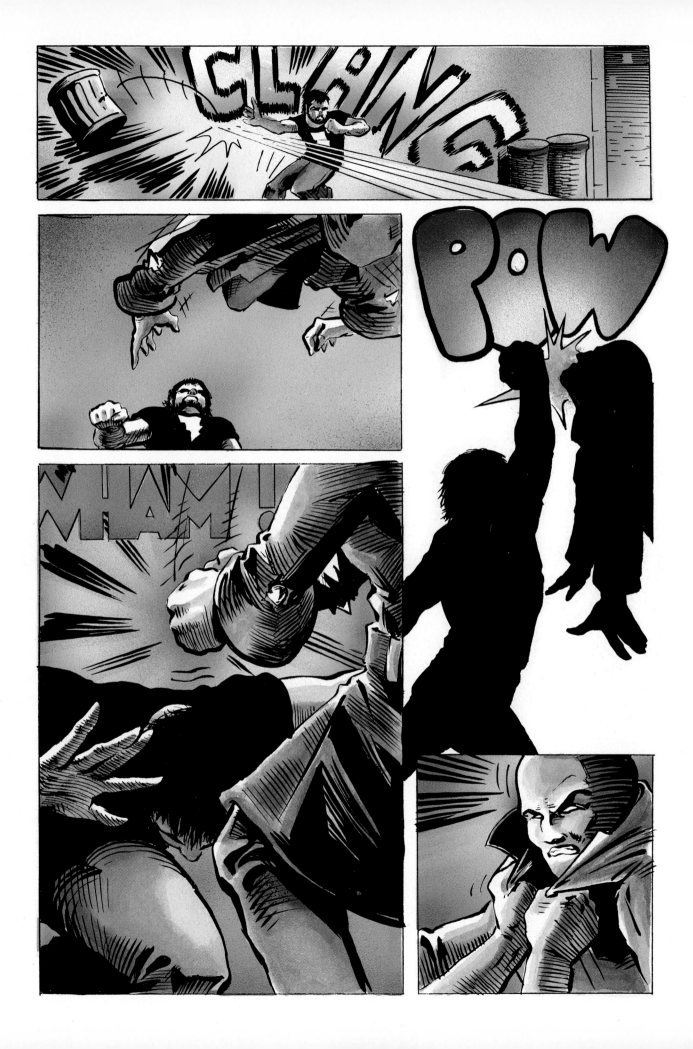

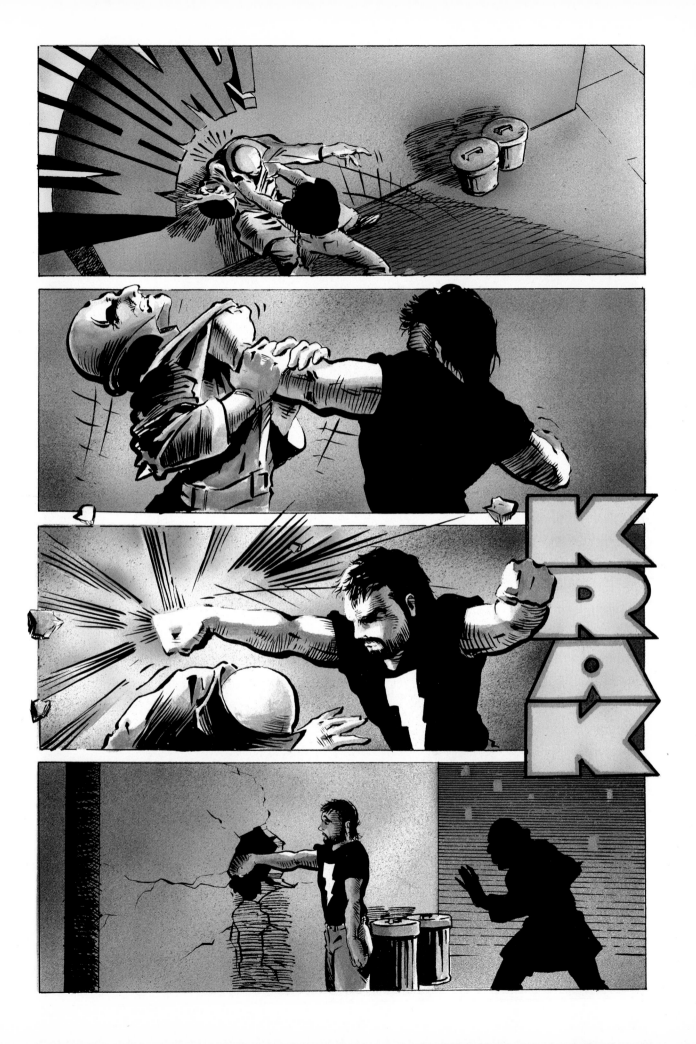

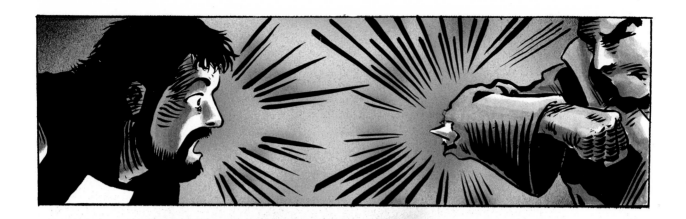

I'D LIKE TO REPORT A DEATH. A MAN. HE'S IN AN ALLEY WAY OFF SOUTH STREET, BETWEEN 12th AND 13th.

NO, I DON'T KNOW WHO HE IS.

YES, HE WAS BEATEN *VERY* BADLY.

NO. NO. I DIDN'T SEE THE ASSAILANT.

GOD, I SHOULD'VE SAID SOMETHING. BUT WHAT? WHO WOULD BELIEVE THAT- THAT... *WHATEVER IT WAS* REALLY EXISTS.

AND WHAT I DID TO THAT WALL... I WAS *THERE* AND I DON'T BELIEVE.

KEVIN MATCHSTICK, YOU ARE EITHER A BITTER, BITTER CYNIC OR A RAVING LOON.

BRINNGG!

YES?

HE'S DEAD? GOOD. WHAT? MATCHSTICK? WAS THE POWER WITH HIM?

DAMN! THEN HE MUST HAVE ALREADY ENCOUNTERED THE WORLD MAGE.

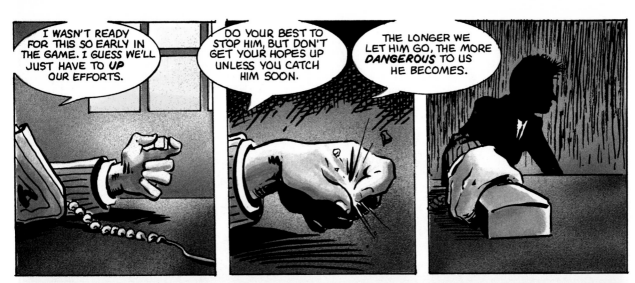

AND CERTAIN FEELINGS THAT OVERTOOK YOU AND SPURRED YOU ON, FEELINGS YOU HAVE NO EXPLANATION FOR.

HOW DO YOU KNOW THIS?! WHAT THE HELL IS HAPPENING HERE?!

YES, I KNOW YOU HAVE MANY QUESTIONS. ASK THEM ONE AT A TIME. I WILL ANSWER SOME OF THEM.

TO START WITH, JUST WHAT OR WHO IS GRACKLEFLINT?

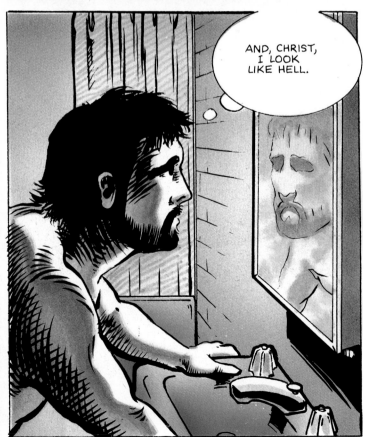

THE HERO DISCOVERED

MAGE™

CHAPTER 2

Too, Too
Solid Flesh

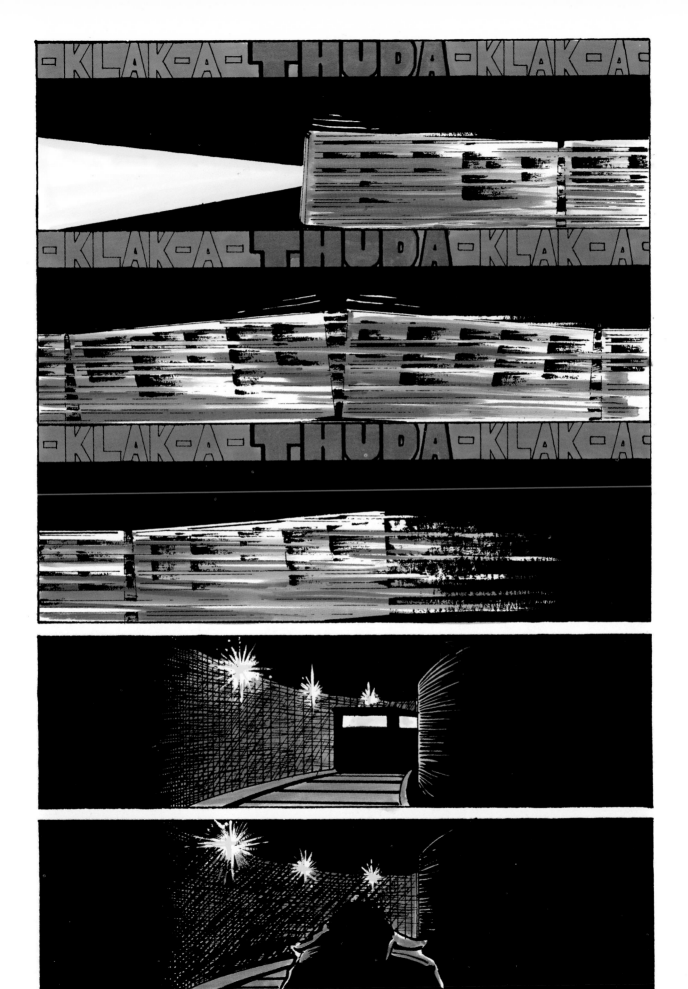

DON'T BE SO SURE HE'S DEAD. ALTHOUGH HE PROBABLY DOESN'T REALIZE WHO HE REALLY IS...

...LET'S MAKE SURE THAT *WE* DON'T FORGET. MOST LIKELY, THE TRAIN BARELY *FAZED* HIM.

WELL, *EMIL* AND *LAZLO* ARE WATCHING THE TWO STOPS THAT BORDER THE AREA WHERE HE WAS HIT.

IF HE COMES OUT THERE, THEY'LL SEE HIM.

BUT I STILL FIND IT HARD TO BELIEVE THAT A SUBWAY TRAIN AT FULL SPEED COULDN'T...

I KNOW, *PIET,* AND AT ONE TIME IT *WOULD'VE* DONE THE JOB. BUT ONCE HE ENCOUNTERED THE *WORLD MAGE,* THE POWER AWAKENED SWIFTLY IN HIM.

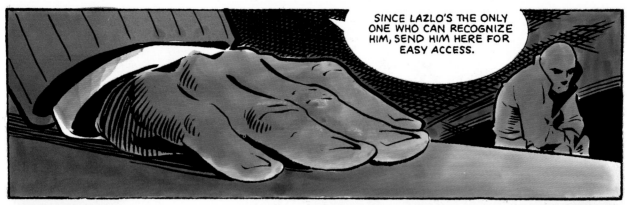

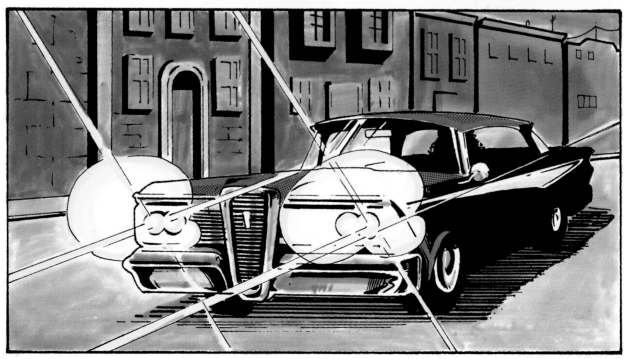

OKAY, HOW DO I EXPLAIN THIS? THIS MORNING I GET HIT BY A SUBWAY TRAIN– NOT A SCRATCH. THIS AFTERNOON– I GET A *SPLINTER!*

WELL, PUT SIMPLY, KEVIN, THE POWER IS YOU, BUT *YOU* ARE NOT *IT*.

BOY, I BET THEY'D JUST LOVE YOU OVER AT *READER'S DIGEST*.

WHAT I MEAN IS THAT THE POWER RISES TO WHATEVER SITUATION, BUT *ONLY* WHEN *IT* FEELS IT'S NEEDED.

I'M AFRAID, MY FRIEND, THAT YOU *CAN'T* CONTROL IT.

JOY.

BOY, I BET THEY'D JUST LOVE YOU OVER AT *READER'S DIGEST*.

THE GRACKLEFLINTS, THOUGH, ARE NOT THE ACTUAL THREAT.

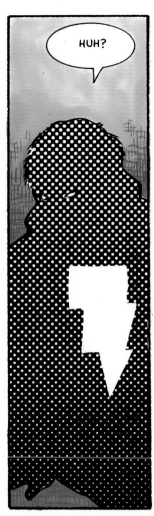

HUH?

THEY ARE MERELY LIEUTENANTS, CONTROLLED BY A GREATER EVIL. A VAST DARKNESS— *THE UMBRA SPRITE.*

WHAT SPRITE?

UMBRA SPRITE. THE GRACKLEFLINTS ARE BROTHERS, AND *HE* IS *THEIR FATHER!* ALTHOUGH HE DOES NOT APPEAR AS HIDEOUS AS THEY, HE IS *FAR* DEADLIER. HE IS ATTILA, HEROD, NERO, HITLER, AND STALIN REALIZED AS ONE.

HIS PLOTTINGS ARE SUBTLE OR DIRECT AS NEEDS BE, BUT THEY ARE ALWAYS INSIDIOUS. HE STRIVES EVEN NOW TO DESTROY WHAT IS LIGHT AND GOOD IN US ALL.

GET *DOWN* HERE, BEFORE SOMEONE SEES YOU!

NO ONE CAN SEE ME UNLESS I WANT THEM TO.

OH.

SO, TELL ME, WHY IS SOMEONE WITH ALL THE POWER YOU CONTAIN...

HEY!

...*SCARED OF HEIGHTS?* I'M SORRY, BUT I FIND IT ALL QUITE SILLY TO...

-URK!

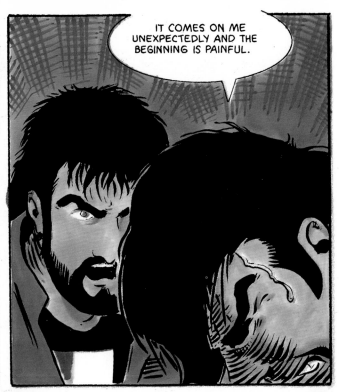

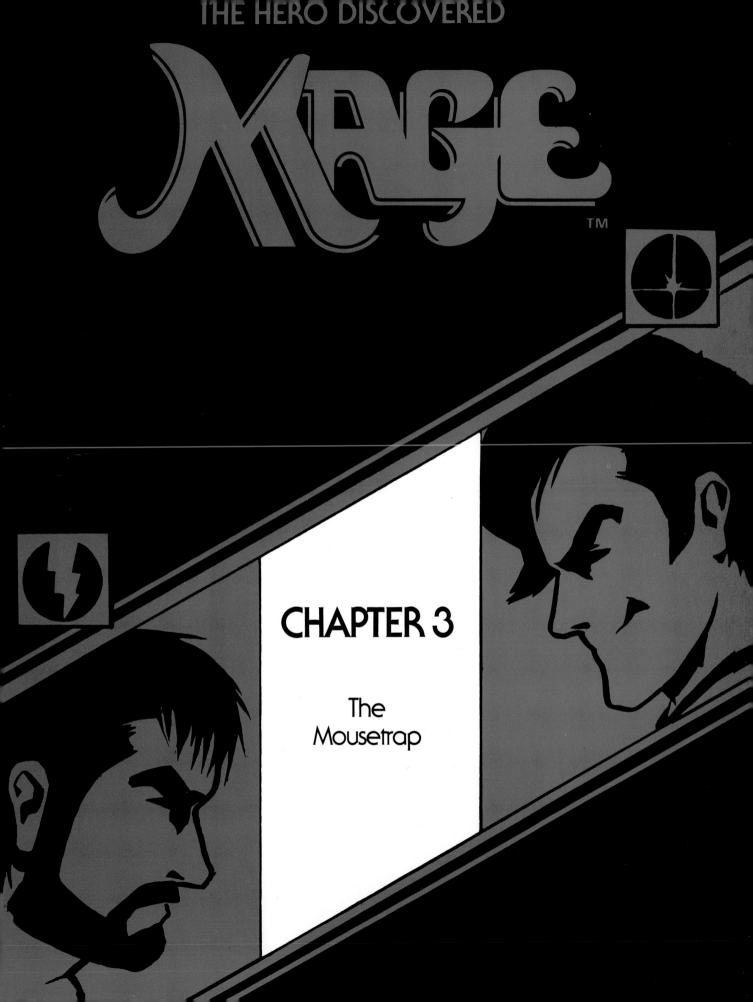

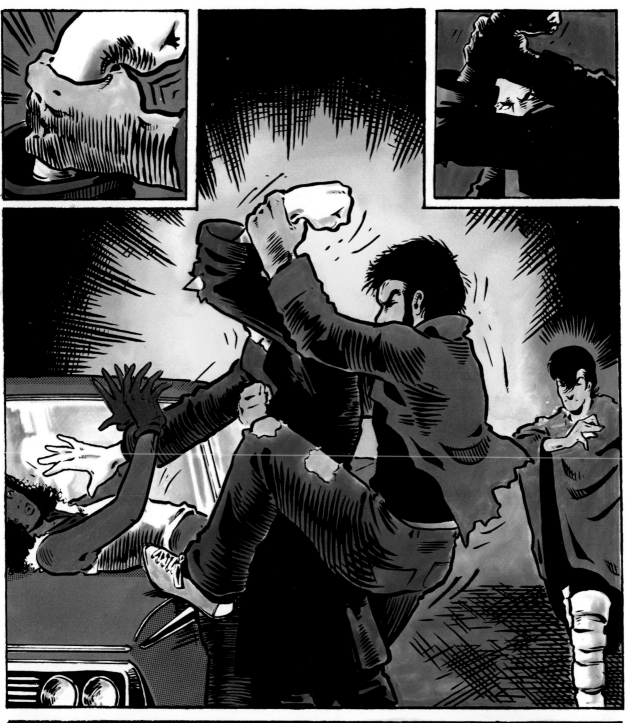

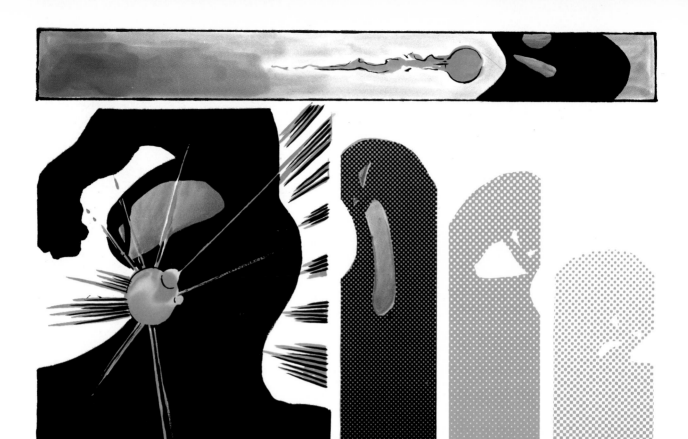

HEY, DRAPES...

THAT WAS A CUTE LITTLE TRICK, BUT AREN'T YOU FORGETTING THE *STAR OF OUR SHOW* OVER HERE?

OH, HE'S ALL RIGHT.

OH, RIGHT! I'M SURE HE'S JUST GREAT! HE ONLY FELL ABOUT *FIVE OR SIX* STORIES!

YOUNG LADY, I *ASSURE* YOU, HE'S JUST FINE!

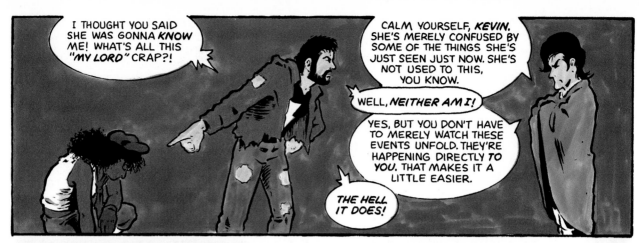

I THOUGHT YOU SAID SHE WAS GONNA *KNOW* ME! WHAT'S ALL THIS *"MY LORD"* CRAP?!

CALM YOURSELF, *KEVIN*. SHE'S MERELY CONFUSED BY SOME OF THE THINGS SHE'S JUST SEEN JUST NOW. SHE'S NOT USED TO THIS, YOU KNOW.

WELL, *NEITHER AM I!*

YES, BUT YOU DON'T HAVE TO MERELY WATCH THESE EVENTS UNFOLD. THEY'RE HAPPENING DIRECTLY *TO YOU.* THAT MAKES IT A LITTLE EASIER.

THE HELL IT DOES!

WE CAN CONTINUE THIS ELSEWHERE, MY FRIEND. RIGHT NOW I SUGGEST THAT YOU GET THE YOUNG LADY'S CAR DOWN OFF THAT CINDER BLOCK SO THAT WE CAN HURRY OUT OF HERE IN A MORE *CONVENTIONAL METHOD* THAN HOW WE ARRIVED.

ALL RIGHT. ALL RIGHT. THAT *POPPIN'* IN AND OUT MAKES ME NAUSEOUS ANYWAY.

AND NOW THERE'S SOMETHING I MUST DISCUSS WITH YOU, YOUNG LADY.

IT SEEMS OUR FRIEND OVER THERE IS ALMOST *TOTALLY* IGNORANT OF *WHO HE REALLY IS.*

BUT...HE...HE *MUST* BE TOLD... HE...

NO!

IMAGINE, IF YOU CAN, HOW *YOU* WOULD FEEL UPON DISCOVERING PRACTICALLY *EVERYTHING* YOU HAD EVER BELIEVED ABOUT YOUR- SELF TO BE *A LIE.*

LOOK AT ME.

I SAID, *LOOK AT ME!* IF YOU RECOGNIZE *HIM,* THEN SURELY YOU KNOW ME.

YES, BUT... BUT I...

MY COUNSEL HAS ALWAYS BEEN WISE TO HIM *IN THE PAST,* HAS IT NOT? THEN TRUST ME IN THIS.

I ASSURE YOU THAT WHEN THE TIME COMES FOR HIM TO KNOW, *YOU* WILL BE THE CAUSE OF IT!

STANIS! LAZLO! WHERE'S FATHER?

IN HIS STUDY... *RECUPERATING*.

RECUPERATING?! FROM WHAT?

I HAD A LITTLE RUN-IN WITH *KEVIN MATCHSTICK* AND *THE MAGE*.

WE'VE HAD SOME TROUBLE, *EMIL*.

THINGS WERE GOING BADLY, SO I WAS FORCED TO CALL ON FATHER'S *SHADE* FOR HELP.

MIRTH ZAPPED HIM PRETTY GOOD.

MORON!

SMACK

HOW IS HE?

I HAVE ABSOLUTELY NO IDEA.

WELL, WHAT WAS I SUPPOSED TO DO?

CALM YOURSELVES. YOUR CONCERN IS APPRECIATED BUT UNNECESSARY. IT WAS A TROUBLESOME BOLT THAT BANISHED MY SHADE, BUT I HAVE RETRIEVED IT AND ALL IS WELL. MERELY SOMEWHAT TIRING.

I'M PLEASED YOU'RE WELL, SIR.

AND I BRING POSSIBLE NEWS OF THE *FISHER KING!* ONE OF OUR CRONIES ON 13th STREET SAID HE SAW A *CRIPPLE* HANGING OUT AROUND THE MID-TOWN DELI EARLIER TODAY. SAID HE'D NEVER SEEN HIM ON THAT TURF BEFORE.

HMM. YES, THESE STREET DWELLERS *DO* TEND TO STICK TO THEIR OWN LITTLE TERRITORIES, DON'T THEY? VERY WELL.

LAZLO, GO CHECK THIS OUT.

SEE IF IT'S *HIM*.

SNAP!

FSS

WE MAY JUST GET LUCKY.

I'LL HAVE TO TOUCH HIM TO BE SURE. WHAT IF IT'S NOT?

KLLA-KUNK!

WHY HERE?

PRIVACY. I FIGURED WE COULD USE A PLACE TO TALK AND THERE'S NO EVENT OR ANYTHING SCHEDULED TONIGHT SO...

GOOD IDEA, *EDSEL.*

I KNOW.

KEVIN, IF I MIGHT MAKE A SUGGESTION. YOUR ACTIVITIES OF LATE HAVE LEFT YOUR APPEARANCE A BIT ON THE SEEDY SIDE.

IN SHORT, YOU LOOK LIKE HELL.

I CAN HELP.

NOW, OBSERVE.

INSTANT...

FIX-IT!

WOW! THAT'S NEAT!

EVER THOUGHT OF SHOWING THAT THING TO *RONCO* OR *K-TEL*? THEY'D *LOVE* IT!

NAH, DAMN THING CAN'T DO *JULIENNE FRIES!*

AND, NOW, MY FRIENDS, WE MUST DISCUSS THE EVENTS THAT HAVE LED TO THE FORMATION OF THIS LITTLE COMPANIONSHIP.

TONIGHT, *EDSEL*, YOU ENCOUNTERED ONE OF THE *GRACKLEFLINTS*. THEY ARE, AS YOU HAVE SAID, QUITE TOUGH AND *VERY* DANGEROUS. THAT *SPUR* YOU SAW ON HIS ELBOW IS *HIGHLY VENOMOUS!*

THANKS.

THERE ARE *FIVE* SUCH CREATURES IN THIS WORLD AND THEY ARE LED BY THEIR FATHER, THE *UMBRA SPRITE.*

MMM– NICE NIGHT.

WELL, WHAT DO THEY WANT?

AH YES, WHAT DO THEY WANT...

WELL, TRADITIONALLY IN THE LONG LEGACY OF THE ETERNAL STRUGGLE, *THE DARKNESS* HAS ALWAYS FOUND A WAY TO PERMEATE SOMEWHAT INTO MANY AREAS AND MANY EVENTS, WHEREAS *THE LIGHT* HAS USUALLY SEEN FIT TO PINPOINT ITS EMBODI-MENTS IN A MORE SPECIFIC MANNER. ONE OF THE GREATEST VESSELS FOR THE LIGHT HAS BEEN A MAN KNOWN AS *THE FISHER KING*. IT IS *HE* THEY WANT, AND *HE* WE MUST PROTECT.

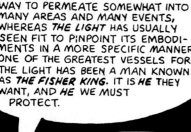

I HAVE NO IDEA.

GREAT.

AND JUST WHERE IS THIS *FISHER KING*?

THINK HOW MUCH HARDER IT USUALLY IS TO NOTICE SOMEONE'S GOOD POINTS RATHER THAN HIS FAULTS. SO IT IS WITH THE *FISHER KING*.

AS AN EMBODIMENT OF GOODNESS, HE IS DIFFICULT TO RECOGNIZE. HE *CHANGES HIS SHAPE* AT WILL AND SO KEEPS US SEARCHING. AS WE SHOULD.

ONE MUST *STRIVE* FOR THE LIGHT. THE DARK WAYS COME FAR TOO EASY.

IT IS DONE.
**THE MARHAULT
IS SUMMONED!**

A STREET-WISE ATTITUDE DOESN'T NECESSARILY MAKE ME A CYNIC.

IN FACT, IF ANYTHING, LIFE ON THE STREETS SERVES TO OPEN YOU UP. WHEN YOU'RE OUT IN THE OPEN, YOU BEGIN TO REALIZE THAT IT *IS* ALL HERE—THE GOOD AND THE BAD, THE CLEAN AND THE DIRTY, THE SOLID AND THE IMAGINARY. IT ALL EXISTS, SO HOW VERY MUCH MORE IS *ALSO* POSSIBLE?

IT'S THE *MIDDLE* CLASSES, TRAPPED INSIDE THEIR TWO-STORY RANCHERS THAT PUT THE IRONCLAD MOLD ON WHAT *CAN* AND *CAN'T* BE.

THE STREETS *LET* YOU BELIEVE.

WELL, I'M SORRY, BUT I'M NOT SO ENCOMPASSING IN MY VIEWS. IT MAY BE INCREDIBLY *BOURGEOIS,* BUT I'M AFRAID I TEND TO STICK TO THE OLD SAYING...

THE HERO DISCOVERED

MAGE™

CHAPTER 4

O What
A Rash And
Bloody Deed

WHAM!

WHAM!

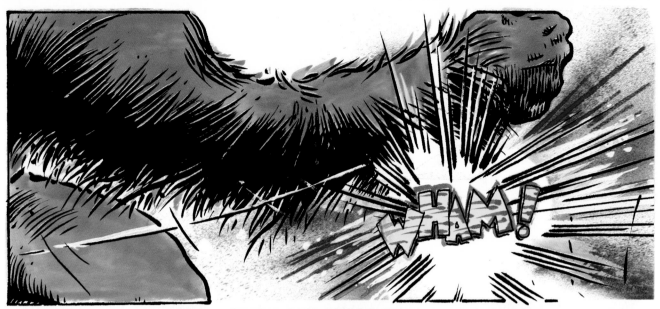

THAT WAS *THE MARHAULT OGRE!*

THE WHAT?

A CREATURE FROM KEVIN'S ...OTHER LIFE!

WELL, WHAT'S IT DOIN' HERE?

THE UMBRA SPRITE MUST'VE SUMMONED IT! I DIDN'T THINK HE COULD.

I'M TOO WEAK. MY POWERS ARE MAINLY SUPPORTIVE, *NOT* COMBATIVE. OH, I CAN ATTACK WHEN I NEED TO, BUT IT'S A STRAIN. THAT FIGHT IN THE ALLEY EMPTIED ME OUT.

BUT I'VE SEEN YOU USE MAGIC SINCE THEN: *HIS CLOTHES, MY BAT...*

THAT WAS NOTHING. MERELY PUSHING ENERGY AROUND HERE AND THERE. *THIS* WOULD TAKE A FULL OFFENSIVE STRIKE.

ESPECIALLY AFTER WHAT I DID TO HIS SHADE!

WELL, GET RID OF IT!

I CAN'T.

WHAT?!

IN FACT MY EARLIER LITTLE ESCAPADES PROBABLY CREATED QUITE A RIPPLE IN THE FIBRES OF THE MAGIC.

THAT'S HOW HE FOUND US. THERE'S NOTHING I CAN DO.

THEN, GET ME MY BAT!!

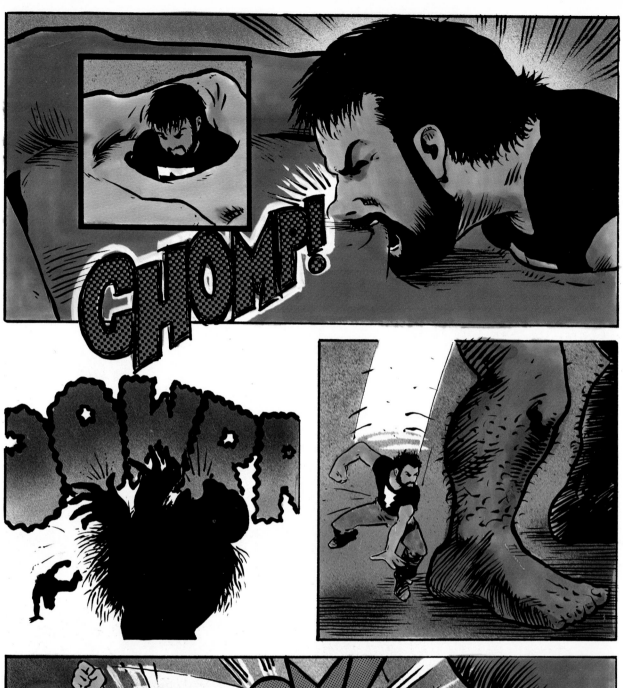

YOU- YOU CAN'T BE SERIOUS! THAT SPELL ISN'T *NEARLY* STRONG ENOUGH TO...

CAN IT, DRAPES! I'M *NOT* GONNA SIT HERE AND WATCH HIM BELT IT OUT WITH THAT THING *ALL ALONE!*

POP!

K'TUNK!

BUT...

NO "BUTS," DRAPES! JUST DO IT!

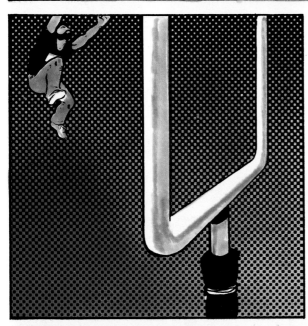

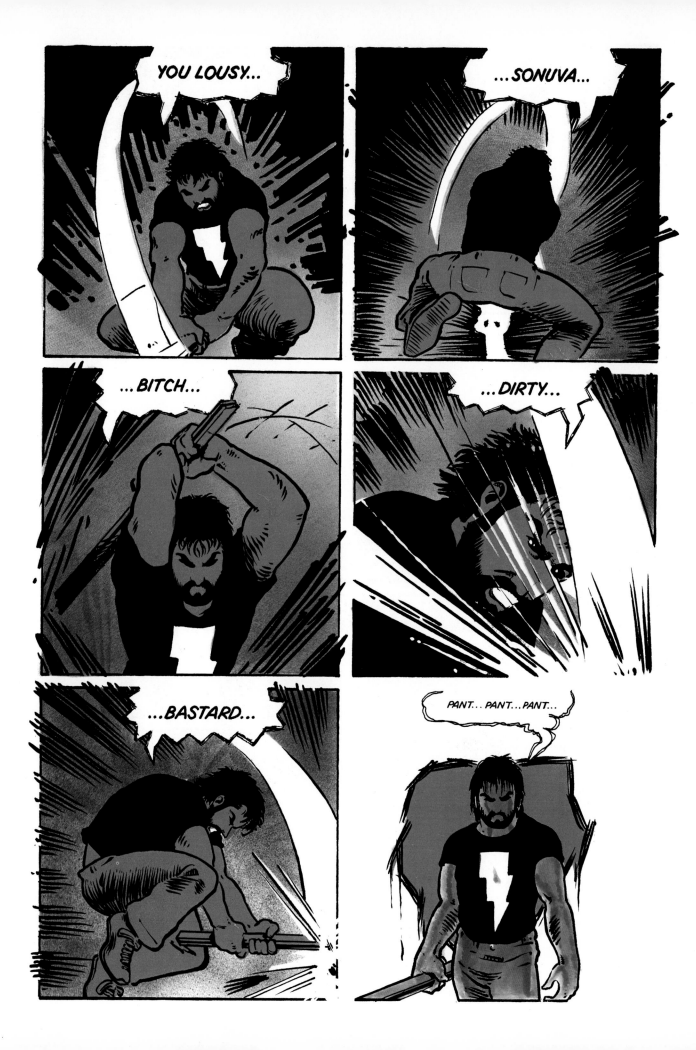

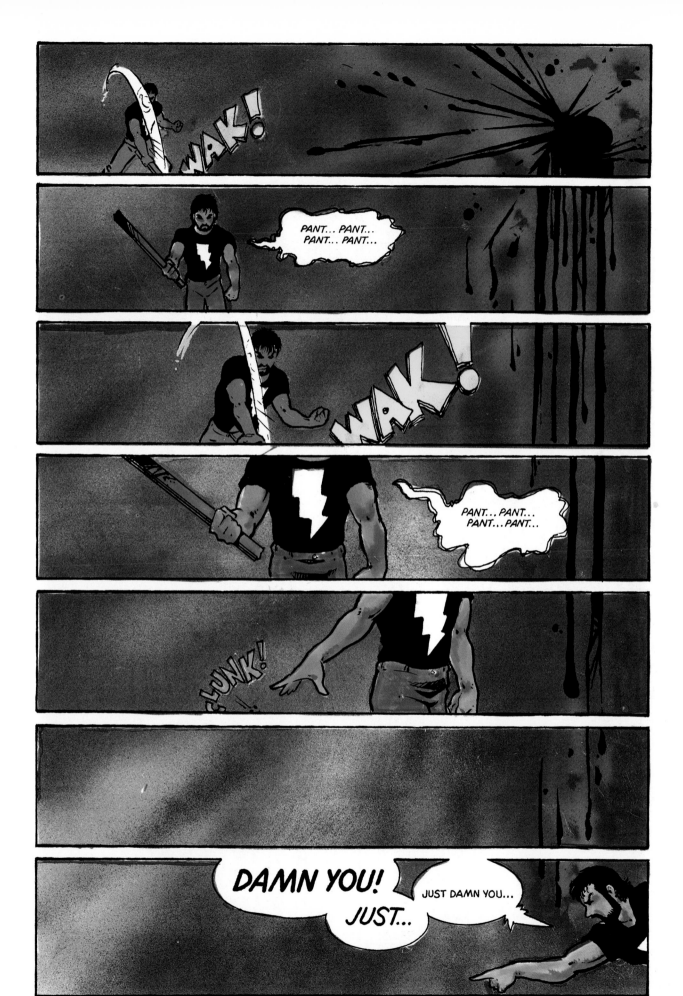

HOW IS SHE?

OUT, BUT FINE. HOW'RE YOU?

LOUSY.

THERE WAS NO OTHER WAY, KEVIN.

I LOST IT.

IT WAS THE ONLY WAY YOU COULD'VE BEATEN HIM.

I...I KILLED HIM.

NO, MY FRIEND—

YOU DIDN'T KILL HIM.

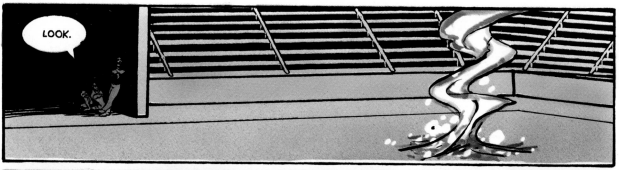

NO, THAT WAS AN *OGRE*, BUT THE FAERIE LANDS ARE MANY AND VARIED. SOME ARE LIGHT AND SOME... *ARE DARK.*

THAT STILL DOESN'T EXCUSE WHAT I DID. *I* DIDN'T KNOW IT COULDN'T BE KILLED.

HELL, I *WANTED* TO KILL IT! AND I SWORE I WOULD *NEVER* DO THAT AGAIN!

YOU SEE, WHEN I WAS A KID, MY DAD BOUGHT ME A PUPPY. HE TOLD ME HER NAME WAS *QUEENIE* AND IT WAS *MY* RESPONSIBILITY TO TRAIN HER AND CARE FOR HER. I COULDN'T HAVE BEEN MORE THAN SIX OR SEVEN BUT, GOD, I LOVED THAT DOG! I WALKED HER *ALL* THE TIME, INSISTED SHE SLEEP IN MY BED, I...

YEAH... WELL, ANYWAY, ONE DAY I WAS TRYIN' TO TEACH HER HOW TO SHAKE HANDS AND SHE JUST COULDN'T GET IT. OF COURSE SHE COULDN'T GET IT. SHE WAS ONLY A COUPLE O' MONTHS OLD. BUT I DIDN'T UNDERSTAND THAT. I LOST MY TEMPER AND STARTED YELLIN' AT HER. THEN, SUDDENLY... SOMEHOW... THERE WAS A STICK IN MY HAND. AND I COULDN'T IMAGINE HOW IT GOT THERE OR WHY I WAS HITTING HER WITH IT. BY THE TIME I WAS ABLE TO STOP... SHE WAS DEAD.

I LOVED HER AND I KILLED HER. I PROMISED MYSELF THAT IT WOULD *NEVER* HAPPEN AGAIN. IF I HAD DONE *THIS*, HOW MUCH WORSE WOULD IT BE AGAINST SOMEONE I WAS REALLY MAD AT? SO ALL MY LIFE, I'VE FOUGHT TO KEEP UNDER CONTROL AND I'VE ALWAYS MANAGED TO REMAIN FAIRLY MODERATE. UNTIL LATELY... *ESPECIALLY* UNTIL TODAY.

YOU WERE A CHILD,
KEVIN, AND BEING A CHILD
MEANS LIVING PURE, UNADULTERATED
EMOTION. WANTS AND NEEDS ARE
ALL A CHILD KNOWS.

AND NOW IT IS
NECESSARY FOR YOU TO
USE THE FERVOR THAT EMOTION
PRODUCES, SO YOUR EMOTIONS
ARE SURFACING *ABOVE* ALL
YOUR WELL-PRACTICED
SELF-RESTRAINT.

OH GREAT.
SO, I'M REVERTING.
BECOMING A CHILD,
AGAIN.

NO, KEVIN,
YOU ARE
BECOMING A
WARRIOR.

WE *ARE* FIGHTING A WAR, YOU KNOW.

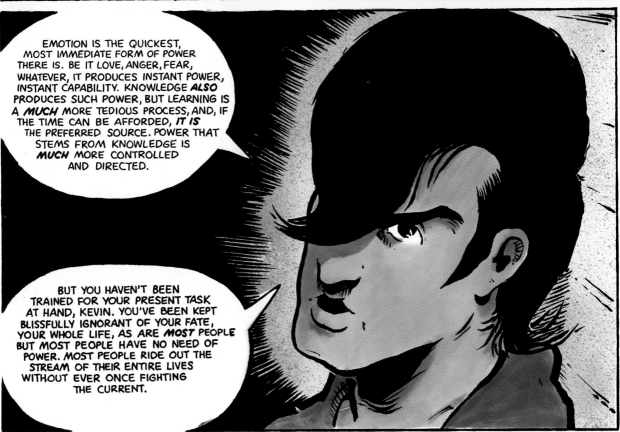

EMOTION IS THE QUICKEST, MOST IMMEDIATE FORM OF POWER THERE IS. BE IT LOVE, ANGER, FEAR, WHATEVER, IT PRODUCES INSTANT POWER, INSTANT CAPABILITY. KNOWLEDGE *ALSO* PRODUCES SUCH POWER, BUT LEARNING IS A *MUCH* MORE TEDIOUS PROCESS, AND, IF THE TIME CAN BE AFFORDED, *IT IS* THE PREFERRED SOURCE. POWER THAT STEMS FROM KNOWLEDGE IS *MUCH* MORE CONTROLLED AND DIRECTED.

BUT YOU HAVEN'T BEEN TRAINED FOR YOUR PRESENT TASK AT HAND, KEVIN. YOU'VE BEEN KEPT BLISSFULLY IGNORANT OF YOUR FATE, YOUR WHOLE LIFE, AS ARE *MOST* PEOPLE BUT MOST PEOPLE HAVE NO NEED OF POWER. MOST PEOPLE RIDE OUT THE *STREAM* OF THEIR ENTIRE LIVES WITHOUT EVER ONCE FIGHTING THE CURRENT.

THEY'RE BORN.

...GET A JOB...

...GROW OLD...

THEY GROW...

...MARRY...

...AND DIE.

AS BILLY PILGRIM WOULD SAY, "SO IT GOES."

AHHH!

MIRTH! YOUR LEG..!

HUH?

OH, I'M SORRY, KEVIN. I FORGOT THAT YOU DIDN'T KNOW. YES, MY LEG WRAPPERS ARE HELD TOGETHER BY A *VERY* POWERFUL SPELL. WELL, WE ALL HAVE WEAKNESSES...

...MINE ARE JUST RATHER SPECIFIC! NOW IN ONE OF MY OTHER LIVES...

OTHER LIVES?!

WE'VE *ALL* HAD OTHER LIVES, KEVIN. I JUST HAPPEN TO REMEMBER ALL MINE.

ANYWAY, AT ONE TIME I HAD A WEAKNESS FOR VERY BEAUTIFUL WOMEN. ≷CHUCKLE≷

"SO IT GOES!"

NOW, IF YOU'LL EXCUSE ME...

AHH! THAT'S BETTER!

MRTH!
WHAT'S WRONG?

ARRGGGH!!

CALM DOWN, KEVIN... UGH... IT'S JUST ANOTHER VISION. I'LL...I'LL BE ALL RIGHT.

THAT'S BETTER. NOW...

DAMN.

APPARENTLY YOUR LITTLE FROLIC WITH THE OGRE MUST'VE SET OFF SOME ALARMS.

WHY?

'CAUSE THERE'RE LOADS OF COPS ON THEIR WAY HERE. LISTEN. YOU SHOULD HEAR THEM SOON.

WRRRRREEEEEEE

THERE.

THE HERO DISCOVERED

CHAPTER 5

Rosencrantz
and
Guildenstern

SUPER-HERO?

YOU'RE A WHAT?

A...UM... A SUPER-HERO.

Y'MEAN CAN'T BE HURT, STRONGER'N HELL, —DAT SORTA THING...

YEAH.

HOW 'BOUT FLYIN'?

CAN Y'FLY?

GOD, I HOPE NOT.

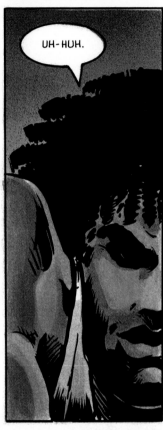

UH-HUH.

WELL, WHAT ABOUT Y'LITTLE PAL-DA MAGICIAN.

THE MAGE. MIRTH.

YEAH-UH-HUH. WELL WHAT HAPPEN T'HIM?

I TOLD YOU. HE *ISN'T* ANYMORE.

IDN'T WHAT?

I DON'T KNOW-JUST ISN'T. ONE MINUTE HE'S RIGHT IN FRONT OF ME, OPENIN' THE DOOR, AND THE NEXT- IT'S JUST ME, THE GIRL, THE COPS, AND ONE *REALLY* BANGED-UP STADIUM.

HE JUST VANISHED.

Y'KNOW. MAGIC.

MAGIC.
UH-HUH.

SO, THIS GUY'S A BROTHER?

NO.

NO, HE WAS WHITE.

UH-HUH.

Y'KNOW, THERE'RE SOME PEOPLE 'ROUND MIGHT B'LIEVE DOSE WHACKY-SOUNDIN' TALES O' YOURS. THERE'RE SOME THAT KNOWS WHAT MAGIC CAN REALLY DO.

YEAH, *HOODOO'S* SOME POTENT SHIT, MAN. 'CEPT IT TAKES A CERTAIN UNDERSTANDIN'—A CERTAIN SUMTHIN' IN *D'BLOOD*, Y'KNOW. WHITE DUDES—THEY JUST AIN'T GOT D'BLOOD.

SO, THESE PEOPLE WHAT DIG HOODOO—THEY'D PROBABLY SAY YOU'S JUST ONE POOR, CRAZY SHIT.

IT'S TRUE.

UH-HUH.

BUT...

DAMN.

OKAY...

GO AHEAD.

HIT ME.

AS HARD AS YOU CAN.

NONE OF YOU EVEN SEE IT! YOU ALL ACCEPT EVERYTHING HE SAYS. YOU JUST "ASSUME" WE MUST WIN THIS FIGHT.

WHAT IS THE USE OF THAT, THOUGH? WHEN HAS EITHER SIDE HELD VICTORY FOR VERY LONG IN THIS...

AAGH!

GEEZ, EMIL, I DON'T SEE WHY YOU'RE SO UPSET. OF COURSE WE'LL WIN! FATHER'S INFALLIBLE!

I MEAN, HE'S ALWAYS COME THROUGH IN THE PAST, RIGHT?

EMIL?

DISMAL PLACE, THIS.

WELL, IT AIN'T ASPEN. WHERE THE HELL HAVE YOU BEEN?

OH, I'M AFRAID I *DO* HAVE TO APOLOGIZE FOR THAT. REMEMBER WHEN I TOLD YOU I WAS FEELING SOMEWHAT DRAINED? WELL, MY MAGIC *WAS* QUITE LOW. REAL BORDERLINE TYPE STUFF.

ANYWAY, WHEN WE WERE SURPRISED BY THOSE COPS AT THE DOOR, I QUITE INSTINCTIVELY RAISED THE LAYERS OF MAGICAL DEFENSE AROUND ME.

AND, I'M AFRAID, EVEN THAT WAS TOO MUCH OF A STRAIN. I PASSED OUT. AND WHEN I DID, I JUST NATURALLY SLIPPED INTO ONE OF THE FAERIE LANDS, THERE TO REST UNTIL I RECOVERED.

UNTIL NOW.

BUT I MUST SAY, KEVIN, THAT ALTHOUGH ALLOWING YOURSELF TO BE LOCKED UP *WAS* INDEED A VERY STRATEGIC IDEA...

WELL, LET'S JUST SAY I'M A TRIFLE *SURPRISED* THAT YOU WOULD SUBMIT TO ARREST WITHOUT ANY SORT OF STRUGGLE. YOU *HAVE* BEEN PRONE TO THAT SORT OF THING LATELY, Y'KNOW.

WELL, THERE WASN'T ALL THAT MUCH I COULD'VE DONE...

OH? WHAT ABOUT YOUR POWERS?

LOOKS LIKE I WAS RIGHT.

I KINDA FIGURED THAT WITHOUT YOU *HERE*, THEY WOULDN'T WORK.

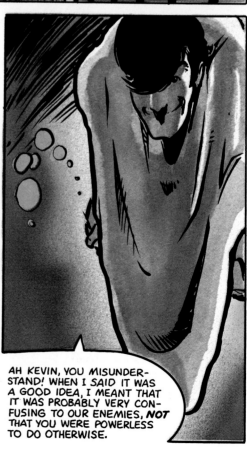

AH KEVIN, YOU MISUNDER-STAND! WHEN I *SAID* IT WAS A GOOD IDEA, I MEANT THAT IT WAS PROBABLY VERY CON-FUSING TO OUR ENEMIES, *NOT* THAT YOU WERE POWERLESS TO DO OTHERWISE.

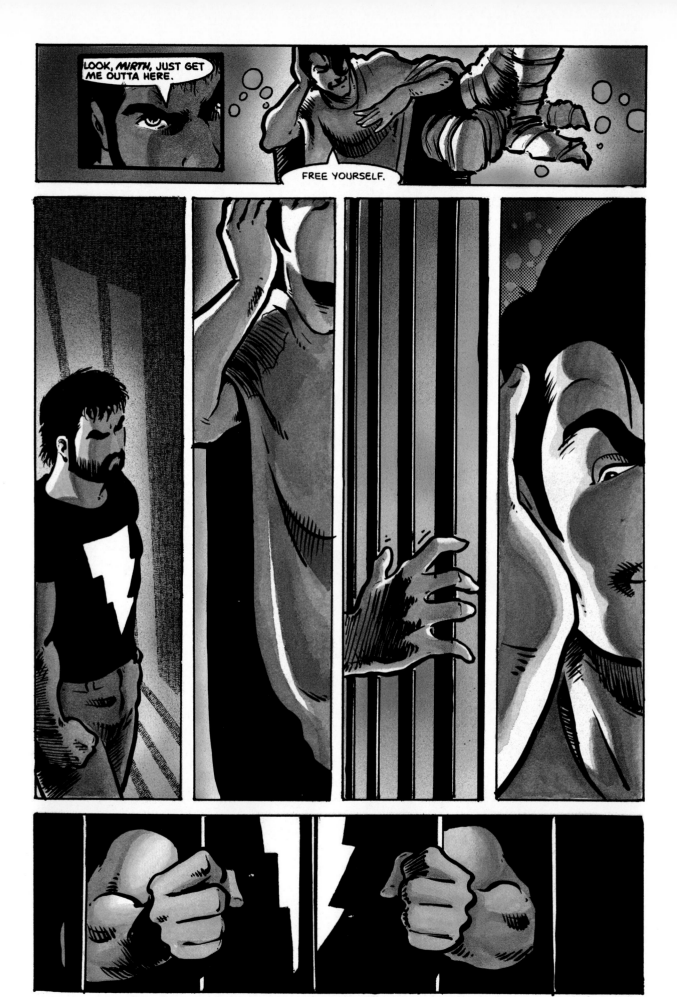

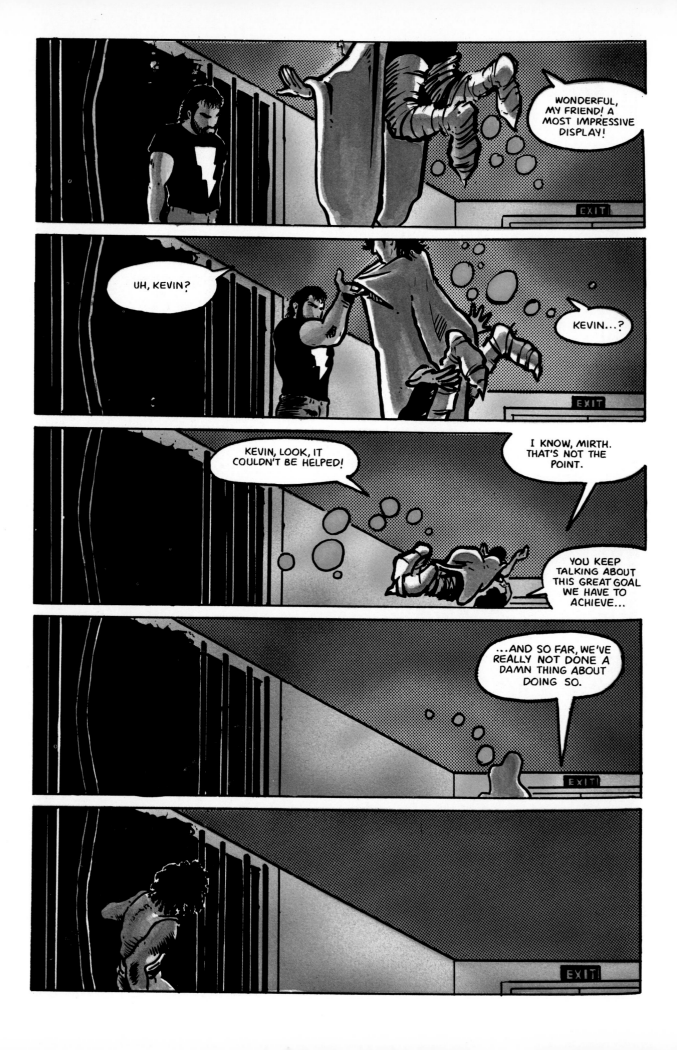

I MEAN, SO FAR, WE'VE ONLY *JUST* BEEN ABLE TO FIGHT OFF THE ATTACKS THE UMBRA SPRITE AND HIS UGLY KIDS HAVE LAUNCHED ON US. *HOW* DO THEY KEEP FINDING US?

A GOOD POINT, KEVIN...

AND I AGREE! IT IS TIME FOR THE QUARRY TO TURN AND FIGHT!

WHAT'S THAT?

OH, JUST A BOUT OF FORGETFULNESS FOR YOUR FRIENDS *IN* THE CELL.

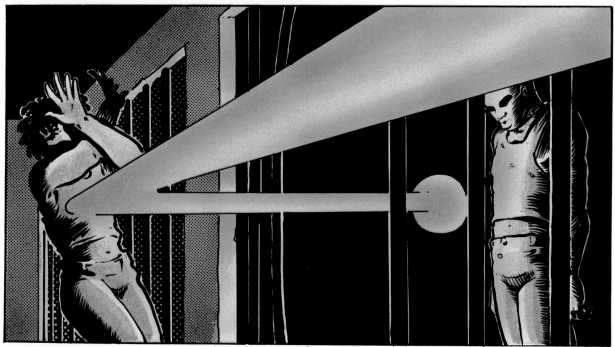

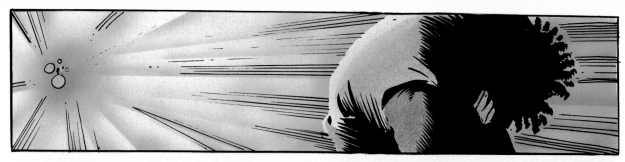

RASHEM!

HEY MAN, LIKE HOW'D YOU GET OUT THERE?

C'MON, RASH, LET ME OUT, TOO!

YOU... DON'T REMEMBER...

REMEMBER WHAT?

C'MON, MAN, LEMME OUT!

RASHEM!

RASHEM?

I SUPPOSE *THEY* WON'T REMEMBER ANYTHING, EITHER.

THEY DON'T EVEN SEE US! WE TREAD ON THE VERY BORDERS OF ONE OF THE FAERIE LANDS, AND SO ARE *OUTSIDE* THEIR FRAME OF TIME REFERENCE.

BUT WE CAN STILL SEE THEM. WOW, THAT'S CREEPY.

EH, YOU GET USED TO IT. NOW, LET'S SEE...

HERE WE GO.

AND NOW THEY'LL EVEN HAVE *NO* RECORD OF THEIR LOST MEMORIES.

OH YUCK, KEVIN, *LOUSY* PICTURE.

SEE, SINCE SHE'S A MINOR, *HER FATHER* INSISTED ON THE KIDNAPPING CHARGE YOU GOT TAGGED WITH. *THAT'S* OUR NEXT PROBLEM...

CLICK-CLICK!

ALL RIGHT, KEVIN, YOU AND YOUR FRIEND HOLD IT RIGHT THERE!

AND NO SUDDEN MOVES, I'VE GOT A GUN!

OKAY, KEVIN, WHAT THE HELL'S GOING ON HERE? WHY'S EVERYONE LOOK LIKE THEY JUST STEPPED OUTTA *THE TWILIGHT ZONE*, AND JUST WHAT HAVE YOU TWO GOT TO DO WITH IT?

SEAN?!

HOW COME HE'S MOVIN'?

DON'T KNOW.

THEN LET ME HANDLE THIS.

OKAY.

DON'T COME ANY CLOSER, KEVIN.

I...I MEAN IT!

LOOK, SEAN, WHEN WE TALKED EARLIER, YOU SAID YOU WANTED TO HELP ME. YOU WANTED ME TO OPEN UP AND TELL YOU EVERYTHING THAT'S HAPPENED, WHY I WAS AT THAT STADIUM. WELL, LISTEN TO ME NOW, SEAN. THERE ARE FORCES AT WORK HERE THAT YOU CAN'T UNDERSTAND, YET.

BUT, BELIEVE ME, THESE PEOPLE ARE SAFE AND YOU SHOULDN'T EVEN BE HERE. IN FACT, THIS ISN'T EVEN A *HERE*— IT'S A *WHEN*— KINDA LIKE A MOMENT PLUCKED OUTTA TIME. BELIEVE ME, WE WANT TO HELP.

WELL, WHO'S HE?

YOUR FRIEND.

OH, Y'MEAN *MIRTH?* SEAN, IF ANYONE CAN EXPLAIN THIS WHOLE MESS, IT'S HIM!

MIRTH, THIS IS *SEAN KNIGHT.* HE'S THE PUBLIC DEFENDER THAT'S BEEN TRYING TO HELP ME. BUT I'M AFRAID I WASN'T TOO GENEROUS WITH THE INFORMATION JUST THEN.

DO TELL. YES, I KNOW WHO SEAN IS.

I WAS ABLE TO KEEP AN EYE ON MOST EVERYTHING HAPPENING TO YOU WHILE I WAS RECUPER-ATING.

KINDA TV-IN-BED TYPE THING, AS IT WERE.

OH, OF COURSE.

UH, GUYS... I'VE GOT A GUN—REMEMBER?

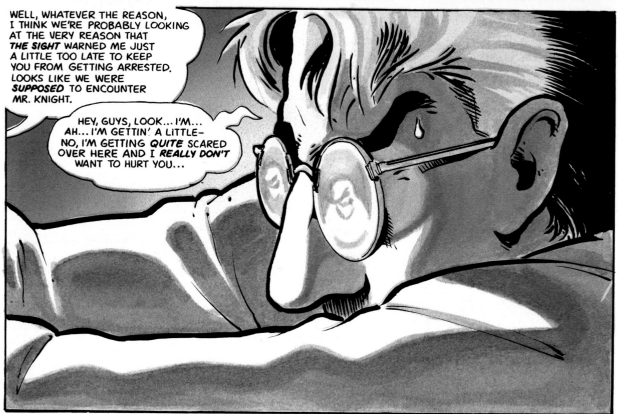